Dedicated to
Peter Newell,
Creator of The Hole Book

THE ARTWORK WAS DONE
USING MIXED MEDIA AND
COLLAGE ON KRAFT PAPER

VIKING
Published by the Penguin Group
Penguin Books USA Inc., 375 Hudson Street, New York, New York 10014, U.S.A.
Penguin Books Ltd, 27 Wrights Lane, London W8 5TZ, England
Penguin Books Australia Ltd, Ringwood, Victoria, Australia
Penguin Books Canada Ltd, 10 Alcorn Avenue, Toronto, Ontario, Canada M4V 3B2
Penguin Books (N.Z.) Ltd, 182-190 Wairau Road, Auckland 10, New Zealand
Penguin Books Ltd, Registered Offices: Harmondsworth, Middlesex, England
First published in 1997 by Viking, a division of Penguin Books USA Inc.

3 5 7 9 10 8 6 4 2
Copyright © Simms Taback, 1997
All rights reserved
Library of Congress Catalog Card Number: 96-61604
ISBN 0-670-86939-2
Printed in China for Harriet Ziefert, Inc.

The Times

OLD LADY
SWALLOWS FLY

There was an old lady who swallowed a fly.

SPIDER'S SOUP

SUPPER **RECIPE:**
1 FLY, 1 HORNET, 2 WASPS
AND 1/2 CATERPILLAR
SAUTÉ IN WORM JUICE UNTIL
DONE AND SERVE.

There was an old lady who swallowed a spider

That wiggled and jiggled and tickled inside her.

There was an old lady who swallowed a bird.

She swallowed the **bird** to catch the spider.

She swallowed the spider to catch the fly.

I don't  *know why*

she swallowed *the fly.*

Perhaps she'll die. she'll leave us high and dry.

She swallowed the **cat** to catch the **bird**.

She swallowed the **bird** to catch the spider.

she swallowed the **spider** to catch the **fly**.

I don't  know why

She swallowed **the fly**.

Perhaps she'll **die**. I hope it's a lie

She swallowed the **dog** to catch the **cat.**

She swallowed the **cat** to catch the **bird.**

She swallowed the **bird** to catch the **spider.**

She swallowed the spider   to catch the **fly.**

I don't   *know why*

She swallowed the fly.

Perhaps she'll die.   There's a tear
in my eye.

SMOKY Cheese

Amstel

REAL Sour Cream

BUTTER Sweet Cream & Salted

CHEESE

Amstel

Philadelphia CREAM CHEESE

SERVING THE HEART OF THE CATSKILLS
WOODSTOCK TIMES

WHOLE COW DEVOURED

WILL BE MISSED

2% LOWFAT MILK

MILK

HERSHEY'S MILK CHOCOLATE

I don't know how

MORAL:

Never swallow a horse.

HERE
LIES AN
OLD
LADY

THERE WAS AN OLD LADY WHO SWALLOWED A FLY, a favorite American folk poem, was first heard in the United States in the 1940's. Several different versions from Georgia, Colorado and Ohio were collected for _Hoosier Folklore_ (Dec. 1947), but its true author remains unknown.